The Case of
The Missing Carrots:
A MOOSE-tery

By Ronnie Krauss
Final sketches by Eduardo
Art colorized by Don Bishop

A Division of HarperCollinsPublishers

Captain Kangaroo beamed with excitement as Mr. Greenjeans plucked a treat from the garden.

"They must be long, fat, and *very* orange," the Captain explained, "so that my cake will taste *extra* delicious!"

"Yes siree!" Mr. Greenjeans said. "How about . . .

"these carrots?"
"Perfect!" the Captain said
with a smile.

"Yum-yum!" Mister Moose smacked his lips. "The Captain's baking his fa-MOOSE carrot cake!"

"Can I help, too?" asked Joey.

"Of course," nodded the Captain. "You can peel the three carrots."

"I only see two," Joey said. "Where's the third?"

Captain Kangaroo looked around . . .

"A carrot is missing!"

"Where could the missing carrot be?" Joey wondered.

Mister Moose had an idea. He grabbed a magnifying glass and called Bunny Rabbit.

"It's a MOOSE-tery," Moose announced, plopping a detective hat on Bunny's head. "And we're going to solve it!"

Suddenly, Moose's eyes popped wide open . . .

"I found something!"

Everyone stared at the paw print. "This proves that someone *in this room* took the carrot!" said Mister Moose. He eyed Joey and the Captain with suspicion.

Then Moose gave Bunny a pencil and notepad. "Interview the suspects!" he said.

"Uh-oh!" shouted the Captain.

"MOOSE-t interesting," said Mister Moose . . .

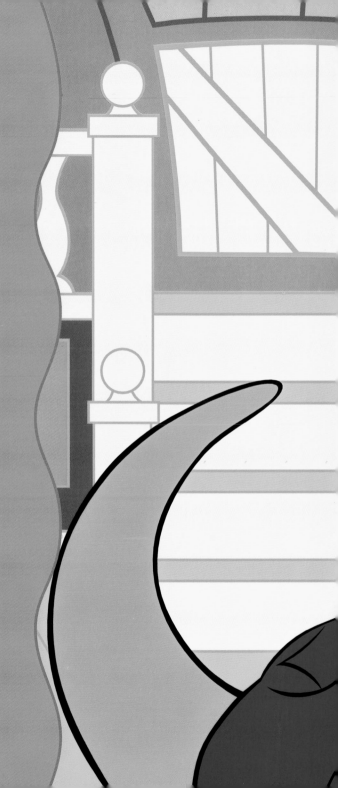

"Nobody move until Bunny makes an official sketch of the scene!" commanded Mister Moose. He turned to his friend—but Bunny Rabbit was not there!

"Now *Bunny* is missing!" Mister Moose exclaimed.

"And that's not all," added Captain Kangaroo. "So is . . .

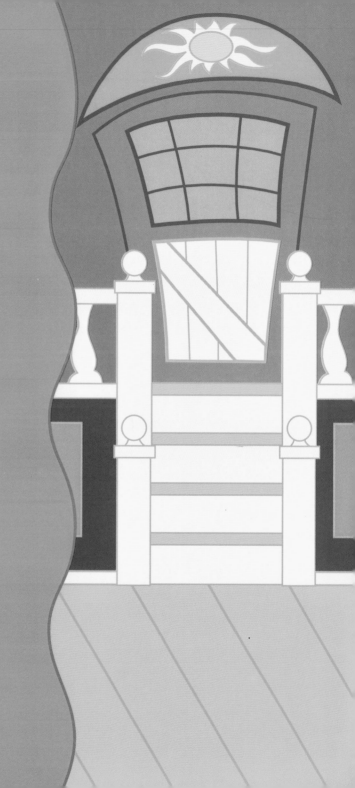

"everything else needed to make a cake!"

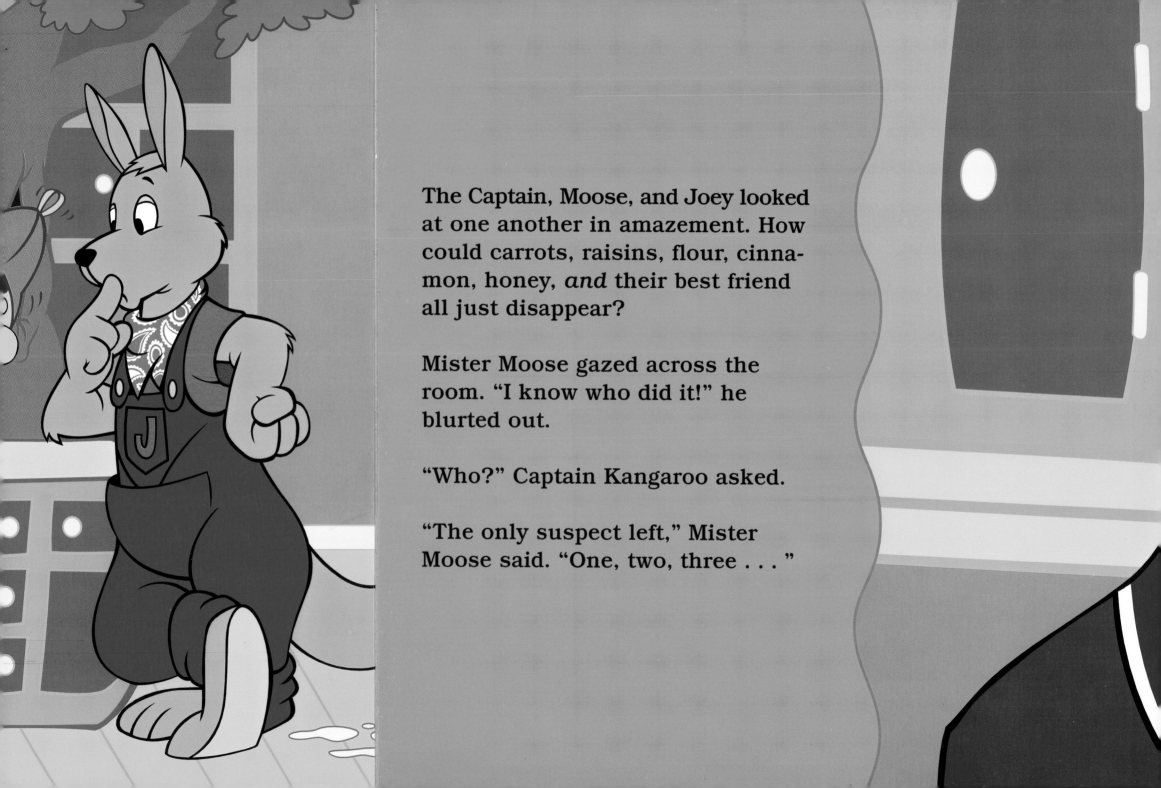

The Captain, Moose, and Joey looked at one another in amazement. How could carrots, raisins, flour, cinnamon, honey, *and* their best friend all just disappear?

Mister Moose gazed across the room. "I know who did it!" he blurted out.

"Who?" Captain Kangaroo asked.

"The only suspect left," Mister Moose said. "One, two, three . . . "

"BUNNY!" finished Mister Moose, as his best friend hopped into the room with something that made everyone cheer.

"My, my!" said Joey. "That looks yummy—but why such a mystery?"

Bunny whispered the answer to Mister Moose.

"Because," Moose repeated . . .

Bunny wants to share his special family recipe with *you*!
Ask a grown-up to help you make it.

Mystery Carrot Cake Supreme

Ingredients:
1 cup canola oil
1½ cups honey
3 eggs
2 cups flour
2 teaspoons cinnamon
2 teaspoons baking soda
2 teaspoons vanilla
1 teaspoon salt
2 cups carrots, shredded
1 cup nuts, chopped
1 cup raisins

Preheat oven to 350 degrees and butter a 9" x 13" pan.
Combine all ingredients in a large bowl and mix well.
Pour mixture into the pan and bake at 350 degrees for
50 minutes.

After cooling, top with whipped cream, vanilla ice cream,
or a cream-cheese icing.

Happy eating!